MANGA SHAKESPEARE®

TWELFTH NIGHT

ADAPTED BY
RICHARD APPIGNANESI

ILLUSTRATED BY
NANA LI

SELF MADE HERO

Published by
SelfMadeHero
A division of Metro Media Ltd
5 Upper Wimpole Street
London W1G 6BP
www.selfmadehero.com

This edition published 2009

Illustrator: Nana Li
Text Adaptor: Richard Appignanesi
Designer: Andy Huckle
Textual Consultant: Nick de Somogyi
Publishing Director: Emma Hayley
With thanks to: Doug Wallace

ISBN: 978-0-9558169-9-4

10 9 8 7 6 5 4 3 2 1
Printed and bound in China

Countess Olivia of Illyria, in mourning for her brother

"We will draw the curtain and show you the picture..."

"If music be the food of love, play on!"

Duke Orsino of Illyria, in love with Olivia

Sir Andrew Aguecheek, a foolish gentleman

"Shall we set about some revels?"

"A plague on these pickle-herring!"

Sir Toby Belch, Olivia's drunken cousin

Malvolio, Olivia's butler

"I'll be revenged
on the whole
pack of you!"

Maria, Olivia's maidservant

"What a caterwauling
do you keep here!"

A Sea-Captain

"This is Illyria, lady..."

Antonio, Sebastian's friend and protector

"His life I gave him, and did thereto add my love..."

Feste, the Fool in Olivia's household

"Many a good hanging prevents a bad marriage!"

"Sportful malice may pluck on laughter!"

Fabian, a servant in Olivia's household

A shipwreck off the coast of Illyria...

THAT STRAIN AGAIN!
IT HAD A DYING FALL!

WILL YOU GO HUNT, MY LORD?

WHAT, CURIO?

THE HART.

IF THE DUKE CONTINUE THESE FAVOURS TOWARDS YOU, CESARIO, YOU ARE LIKE TO BE MUCH ADVANCED.

HE HATH KNOWN YOU BUT THREE DAYS, AND ALREADY YOU ARE NO STRANGER.

IS HE INCONSTANT, SIR, IN HIS FAVOURS?

NO, BELIEVE ME.

I THANK YOU.

HERE COMES THE COUNT.

SAY I DO SPEAK WITH HER, MY LORD —

WHAT THEN?

O, THEN UNFOLD THE PASSION OF MY LOVE.

SURPRISE HER WITH DISCOURSE OF MY DEAR FAITH.

SHE WILL ATTEND IT BETTER IN THY YOUTH.

I THINK NOT SO, MY LORD.

DEAR LAD, BELIEVE IT.

FOR THEY SHALL BELIE THY YEARS THAT SAY THOU ART A MAN.

DIANA'S LIP IS NOT MORE SMOOTH.

THY SMALL PIPE IS AS THE MAIDEN'S ORGAN.

AND ALL IS SEMBLATIVE A WOMAN'S PART.

PROSPER WELL IN THIS, AND THOU SHALT LIVE AS FREELY AS THY LORD, TO CALL HIS FORTUNES THINE.

I'LL DO MY BEST TO WOO YOUR LADY.

YET, WHOEVER I WOO, MYSELF WOULD BE HIS WIFE.

THAT IF ONE BREAK, THE OTHER WILL HOLD.

OR IF BOTH BREAK, YOUR GASKINS FALL.

VERY APT!

IF SIR TOBY WOULD LEAVE DRINKING, THOU WERT AS WITTY A PIECE OF EVE'S FLESH AS ANY IN ILLYRIA.

HERE COMES MY LADY.

MAKE YOUR EXCUSE WISELY, YOU WERE BEST.

SLAM

GOD BLESS THEE, LADY!
TAKE THE FOOL AWAY.
DO YOU NOT HEAR, FELLOWS? TAKE AWAY THE LADY.
SIR, I BADE THEM TAKE AWAY YOU.
MISPRISION IN THE HIGHEST DEGREE!
GOOD MADONNA, GIVE ME LEAVE TO PROVE YOU A FOOL.

I KNOW HIS SOUL IS IN HEAVEN, FOOL.

THE MORE FOOL YOU TO MOURN FOR YOUR BROTHER'S SOUL, BEING IN HEAVEN.

TAKE AWAY THE FOOL, GENTLEMEN.

WHAT THINK YOU OF THIS FOOL, MALVOLIO?

I MARVEL YOUR LADYSHIP TAKES DELIGHT IN SUCH A BARREN RASCAL.

I SAW HIM PUT DOWN THE OTHER DAY WITH AN ORDINARY FOOL THAT HAS NO MORE BRAIN THAN A STONE.

NOW YOU SEE, SIR, HOW YOUR FOOLING GROWS OLD, AND PEOPLE DISLIKE IT.

THOU HAST SPOKE FOR US, MADONNA, FOR HERE COMES...

ONE OF THY KIN.

SHUFFLE

SHUFFLE

HALF DRUNK!

BURP!

POP

POP

A PLAGUE ON THESE PICKLE-HERRING!

"LECHERY"?

I DEFY LECHERY.

SMACK

COUSIN, HOW HAVE YOU COME SO EARLY BY THIS LETHARGY?

THERE'S ONE AT THE GATE.

AY, MARRY, WHAT IS HE?

LET HIM BE THE DEVIL, I CARE NOT!

MADAM, YOND YOUNG FELLOW SWEARS HE WILL SPEAK WITH YOU.

WHAT IS TO BE SAID TO HIM, LADY? HE'S FORTIFIED AGAINST ANY DENIAL.

TELL HIM HE SHALL NOT SPEAK WITH ME.

HAS BEEN TOLD SO, AND HE SAYS HE'LL STAND AT YOUR DOOR LIKE A POST.

WHAT KIND OF MAN IS HE?

THE HONOURABLE LADY OF THE HOUSE...

WHICH IS SHE?

SPEAK TO ME. I SHALL ANSWER FOR HER.

MOST RADIANT, EXQUISITE, AND UNMATCHABLE BEAUTY —

GOOD GENTLE ONE, GIVE ME MODEST ASSURANCE IF YOU BE THE LADY OF THE HOUSE, THAT I MAY PROCEED IN MY SPEECH.

ARE YOU A COMEDIAN?

I HEARD YOU WERE SAUCY AT MY GATES.

IF YOU BE NOT MAD, BE GONE.

IF YOU HAVE REASON, BE BRIEF.

WILL YOU HOIST SAIL, SIR?

HERE LIES YOUR WAY.

NO, I AM TO HULL HERE A LITTLE LONGER.

SPEAK YOUR OFFICE.

MY LORD LOVES YOU.

O, SUCH LOVE COULD BE BUT RECOMPENSED THOUGH YOU WERE CROWNED THE NONPAREIL OF BEAUTY!

HOW DOES HE LOVE ME?

WITH ADORATIONS, FERTILE TEARS,

WITH GROANS THAT THUNDER LOVE,

WITH SIGHS OF FIRE.

YOUR LORD DOES KNOW MY MIND.

I CANNOT LOVE HIM.

YET I KNOW HIM NOBLE, OF GREAT ESTATE, OF STAINLESS YOUTH, FREE, LEARNED AND VALIANT, A GRACIOUS PERSON.

BUT YET I CANNOT LOVE HIM.

HE MIGHT HAVE TOOK HIS ANSWER LONG AGO.

IF I DID LOVE YOU IN MY MASTER'S FLAME WITH SUCH A SUFFERING, IN YOUR DENIAL I WOULD FIND NO SENSE.

I WOULD NOT UNDERSTAND IT.

WHY, WHAT WOULD YOU DO?

MAKE ME A WILLOW CABIN AT YOUR GATE...

AND CALL UPON MY SOUL WITHIN THE HOUSE.

NOT TOO FAST!

HOW NOW? EVEN SO QUICKLY MAY ONE CATCH THE PLAGUE?

METHINKS I FEEL THIS YOUTH'S PERFECTIONS WITH AN INVISIBLE AND SUBTLE STEALTH, TO CREEP IN AT MINE EYES.

WELL, LET IT BE.

WHAT, HO, MALVOLIO!

HE LEFT THIS RING BEHIND HIM.

RUN AFTER THAT MESSENGER.

TELL HIM I'LL NONE OF IT.

DESIRE HIM NOT TO FLATTER HIS LORD, NOR HOLD HIM UP WITH HOPES.

IF THAT THE YOUTH WILL COME THIS WAY TOMORROW, I'LL GIVE HIM REASONS FOR IT.

HIE THEE, MALVOLIO.

MADAM, I WILL.

BY YOUR PATIENCE, NO.

THE MALIGNANCY OF MY FATE MIGHT DISTEMPER YOURS.

I CRAVE YOUR LEAVE THAT I MAY BEAR MY EVILS ALONE.

MY NAME IS SEBASTIAN.

IF THE HEAVENS HAD BEEN PLEASED, WOULD WE HAD SO ENDED! BUT YOU, SIR, TOOK ME FROM THE SEA.

MY SISTER DROWNED.

ALAS THE DAY!

A LADY, IT WAS SAID, MUCH RESEMBLED ME.

SHE IS DROWNED WITH SALT WATER, THOUGH I DROWN HER REMEMBRANCE AGAIN WITH MORE.

LET ME BE YOUR SERVANT.

IF YOU WILL NOT UNDO WHAT YOU HAVE DONE — THAT IS, KILL HIM WHOM YOU HAVE RECOVERED — DESIRE IT NOT.

THE COUNTESS OLIVIA RETURNS THIS RING TO YOU, SIR.

SHE ADDS THAT YOU SHOULD PUT YOUR LORD INTO ASSURANCE SHE WILL NONE OF HIM.

SHE TOOK THE RING OF ME.

I'LL NONE OF IT.

HER WILL IS IT SHOULD BE RETURNED.

IF IT BE WORTH STOOPING FOR, THERE IT LIES.

IF NOT, BE IT HIS THAT FINDS IT.

?

I LEFT NO RING WITH HER. WHAT MEANS THIS LADY?

DUNK

SHE LOVES ME, SURE.

NONE OF MY LORD'S RING?

WHY, HE SENT HER NONE.

TRMP TRMP TRMP

I AM THE MAN!

IF IT BE SO, POOR LADY, SHE WERE BETTER LOVE A DREAM!

TRMP TRMP TRMP

FOR THE LOVE O' GOD, PEACE!

MY MASTERS, ARE YOU MAD?

DO YE MAKE AN ALE-HOUSE OF MY LADY'S HOUSE?

IS THERE NO RESPECT OF PLACE, PERSONS NOR TIME IN YOU?

SCOLDED

BURP

SIR TOBY, MY LADY BADE ME TELL YOU THAT, IF YOU CAN SEPARATE YOURSELF AND YOUR MISDEMEANOURS, YOU ARE WELCOME TO THE HOUSE.

IF NOT, SHE IS VERY WILLING TO BID YOU FAREWELL.

FAREWELL, DEAR HEART, SINCE I MUST NEEDS BE GONE.

GUH

NAY, GOOD SIR TOBY.

SNIFF

ART ANY MORE THAN A STEWARD?

HIS EYES DO SHOW HIS DAYS ARE ALMOST DONE.

DOST THOU THINK, BECAUSE THOU ART VIRTUOUS, THERE SHALL BE NO MORE CAKES AND ALE?

AND GINGER SHALL BE HOT IN THE MOUTH TOO.

74

A STOUP OF WINE, MARIA!

BANG

MISTRESS MARY, IF YOU PRIZED MY LADY'S FAVOUR, YOU WOULD NOT GIVE MEANS FOR THIS UNCIVIL RULE.

SWISH

SHE SHALL KNOW OF IT.

HMPF

SLAM

SWEET SIR TOBY, BE PATIENT FOR TONIGHT.

FOR MONSIEUR MALVOLIO...

SINCE THE YOUTH OF THE COUNT'S WAS TODAY WITH MY LADY, SHE IS MUCH OUT OF QUIET.

LET ME ALONE WITH HIM.

PAT
PAT

TELL US SOMETHING OF HIM.

HE IS A KIND OF PURITAN.

O, IF I THOUGHT THAT, I'D BEAT HIM LIKE A DOG.

WHOOOOOOO
GIVE ME SOME MUSIC.
THAT ANTIQUE SONG WE HEARD LAST NIGHT
METHOUGHT DID RELIEVE MY PASSION MUCH.
HE IS NOT HERE, YOUR LORDSHIP, THAT SHOULD SING IT.
WHOOOO
WHO WAS IT?
FESTE, THE JESTER THAT THE LADY OLIVIA'S FATHER TOOK MUCH DELIGHT IN.
SEEK HIM OUT AND PLAY THE TUNE THE WHILE.

THINE EYE HATH STAYED UPON SOME FAVOUR THAT IT LOVES, HATH IT NOT, BOY?

THOU DOST SPEAK MASTERLY.

A LITTLE, BY YOUR FAVOUR.

WHAT KIND OF WOMAN IS IT?

OF YOUR COMPLEXION.

WHAT YEARS, I'FAITH?

ABOUT YOUR YEARS, MY LORD.

THERE'S FOR THY PAINS.

NO PAINS, SIR. I TAKE PLEASURE IN SINGING.

I'LL PAY THY PLEASURE, THEN.

TRULY, SIR, AND PLEASURE WILL BE PAID, ONE TIME OR ANOTHER.

NOW THE MELANCHOLY GOD PROTECT THEE!

FAREWELL.

BUT DIED THY SISTER OF HER LOVE, MY BOY?

I AM ALL THE DAUGHTERS OF MY FATHER'S HOUSE, AND ALL THE BROTHERS TOO...

AND YET I KNOW NOT.

SIGH

SIR, SHALL I TO THIS LADY?

AY, TO HER IN HASTE.

SAY MY LOVE CAN BIDE NO DENY.

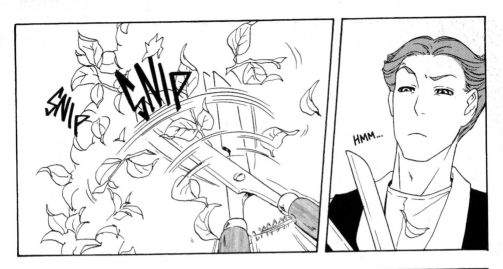

HMM...

SIGNIOR FABIAN!

WOULDST THOU NOT BE GLAD TO HAVE THE RASCALLY SHEEP-BITER COME BY SOME NOTABLE SHAME?

I WOULD EXULT, MAN.

HE BROUGHT ME OUT OF FAVOUR WITH MY LADY ABOUT A BEAR-BAITING HERE.

OUFF

WE WILL FOOL HIM BLACK AND BLUE —

SHALL WE NOT, SIR ANDREW?

FORTUNE, ALL IS FORTUNE.

MARIA ONCE TOLD ME SHE DID AFFECT ME...

AND I HAVE HEARD HERSELF COME THUS NEAR, THAT SHOULD SHE FANCY, IT SHOULD BE ONE OF *MY* COMPLEXION.

HERE'S AN OVERWEENING ROGUE!

O, PEACE! CONTEMPLATION MAKES A RARE TURKEY-COCK OF HIM.

TO BE **COUNT** MALVOLIO —

HAVING BEEN THREE MONTHS MARRIED TO HER, SITTING IN MY VELVET GOWN,

HAVING COME FROM A DAY-BED WHERE I HAVE LEFT OLIVIA...

NOW HE'S DEEPLY IN! LOOK HOW IMAGINATION BLOWS HIM.

SLEEPING.

FIRE AND BRIMSTONE!

AND THEN TO ASK FOR MY KINSMAN TOBY.

BOLTS AND SHACKLES!

...

O, PEACE!

MMF!

I FROWN THE WHILE, AND PERCHANCE WIND UP MY WATCH, OR PLAY WITH SOME RICH JEWEL.

TOBY APPROACHES, CURTSIES THERE TO ME.

SHALL THIS FELLOW LIVE?

WHAT HAVE WE HERE?

BY MY LIFE, THIS IS MY LADY'S HAND.

THESE BE HER VERY C'S, HER U'S AND HER T'S...

AND THUS MAKES SHE HER GREAT P'S...

TO WHOM SHOULD THIS BE?

...

"TO THE UNKNOWN BELOVED..."

'TIS MY LADY.

WHO YOU ARE AND WHAT YOU WOULD ARE OUT OF MY WELKIN.

I MIGHT SAY "ELEMENT"...

BUT THE WORD IS OVERWORN.

BEAM

THIS FELLOW IS WISE ENOUGH TO PLAY THE FOOL.

HE MUST OBSERVE THEIR MOOD ON WHOM HE JESTS.

THIS IS A PRACTICE AS FULL OF LABOUR AS A WISE MAN'S ART.

HUFF

HUFF

TAK

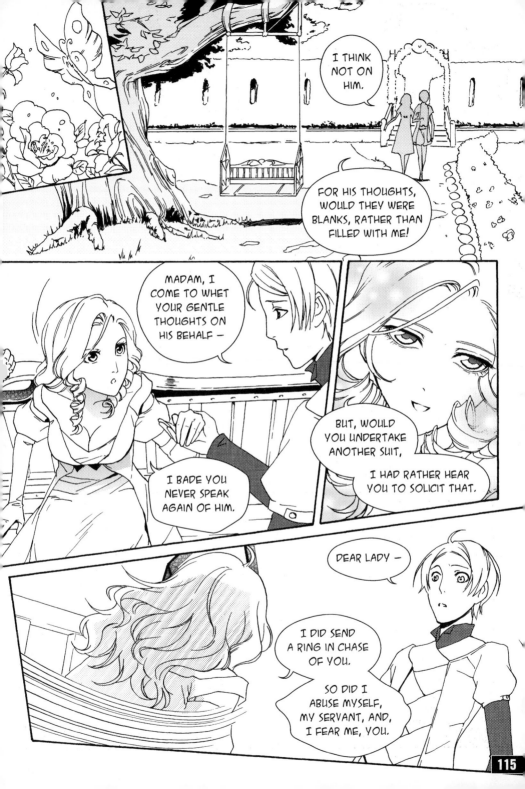

I THINK NOT ON HIM.

FOR HIS THOUGHTS, WOULD THEY WERE BLANKS, RATHER THAN FILLED WITH ME!

MADAM, I COME TO WHET YOUR GENTLE THOUGHTS ON HIS BEHALF —

I BADE YOU NEVER SPEAK AGAIN OF HIM.

BUT, WOULD YOU UNDERTAKE ANOTHER SUIT,

I HAD RATHER HEAR YOU TO SOLICIT THAT.

DEAR LADY —

I DID SEND A RING IN CHASE OF YOU.

SO DID I ABUSE MYSELF, MY SERVANT, AND, I FEAR ME, YOU.

TO FORCE THAT ON YOU, IN SHAMEFUL CUNNING, WHICH YOU KNEW NONE OF YOURS...

WHAT MIGHT YOU THINK?

LET ME HEAR YOU SPEAK.

I PITY YOU.

THAT'S A DEGREE TO LOVE.

NO, FOR 'TIS A VULGAR PROOF THAT VERY OFT WE PITY ENEMIES.

NO, I'LL NOT STAY A JOT LONGER.

THY REASON, GIVE THY REASON.

I SAW YOUR NIECE DO MORE FAVOURS TO THE COUNT'S SERVINGMAN THAN EVER SHE BESTOWED UPON ME.

SHE DID SHOW FAVOUR TO THE YOUTH ONLY TO EXASPERATE YOU.

WILL YOU MAKE AN ASS OF ME?

THUNK
WILL EITHER OF YOU BEAR ME A CHALLENGE TO HIM?
SMACK
GO,
WRITE IT IN A MARTIAL HAND.
LET THERE BE GALL ENOUGH IN THY INK.
CLICK
THOUGH THOU WRITE WITH A GOOSE-PEN, NO MATTER.
ABOUT IT!
NOD
NOD

SIGH

WHERE'S MALVOLIO?

HE IS SAD AND CIVIL, AND SUITS WELL WITH MY FORTUNES.

HE'S COMING, MADAM.

BUT IN VERY STRANGE MANNER.

HE IS SURE POSSESSED.

WHY, DOES HE RAVE?

NO, MADAM, HE DOES NOTHING BUT SMILE.

FOR SURE THE MAN IS TAINTED IN HIS WITS.

SMILEST THOU?

SAD, LADY?

I COULD BE SAD.

THIS DOES MAKE SOME OBSTRUCTION IN THE BLOOD, THIS CROSS-GARTERING.

BUT WHAT OF THAT?

I SENT FOR THEE UPON A SAD OCCASION.

WHAT IS THE MATTER WITH THEE?

NOT BLACK IN MY MIND, THOUGH YELLOW IN MY LEGS.

IT DID COME TO HIS HANDS,

AND COMMANDS SHALL BE EXECUTED.

NO WORSE MAN THAN SIR TOBY TO LOOK TO ME?

THIS CONCURS DIRECTLY WITH THE LETTER...

"LET THIS FELLOW BE LOOKED TO"!

"FELLOW"!

NOT "MALVOLIO".

NOTHING CAN COME BETWEEN ME AND THE FULL PROSPECT OF MY HOPES.

COME, WE'LL HAVE HIM IN A DARK ROOM AND BOUND.

MY NIECE IS ALREADY IN THE BELIEF THAT HE'S MAD.

WE MAY CARRY IT, FOR OUR PLEASURE AND HIS PENANCE...

TILL OUR PASTIME, TIRED OUT, PROMPT US TO HAVE MERCY ON HIM.

HERE'S THE CHALLENGE.

I WARRANT THERE'S VINEGAR AND PEPPER IN IT.

"YOUTH, WHATSOEVER THOU ART, THOU ART BUT A SCURVY FELLOW."

"IF IT BE THY CHANCE TO KILL ME,

THOU KILL'ST ME LIKE A ROGUE AND VILLAIN."

"THY SWORN ENEMY, ANDREW AGUECHEEK."

...

...

GO, SIR ANDREW. SCOUT FOR HIM AT THE CORNER OF THE ORCHARD.

AWAY.

NOW WILL NOT I DELIVER HIS LETTER.

THIS WILL BREED NO TERROR IN THE YOUTH.

HE WILL FIND IT COMES FROM A CLODPOLL.

HERE HE COMES WITH YOUR NIECE.

I WILL MEDITATE UPON SOME HORRID MESSAGE FOR A CHALLENGE.

RITSCH

GO WITH ME TO MY HOUSE, AND HEAR HOW MANY FRUITLESS PRANKS THIS RUFFIAN HATH BOTCHED UP.

THOU SHALT NOT CHOOSE BUT GO. DO NOT DENY.

WOULD THOU BE RULED BY ME?

WHAT IS IN THIS?

I AM MAD, OR ELSE THIS IS A DREAM.

IF IT BE THUS TO DREAM, STILL LET ME SLEEP!

DRIP

DROP

TREMBLE

THEY KEEP ME IN DARKNESS, SEND MINISTERS TO ME —

ASSES!

THEN YOU ARE MAD INDEED, IF YOU BE NO BETTER IN YOUR WITS THAN A FOOL.

MALVOLIO, THY WITS THE HEAVENS RESTORE!

SIR TOPAS!

WHO, I, SIR? NOT I, SIR.

GOD BE WITH YOU, GOOD SIR TOPAS.

MARRY, AMEN.

FOOL, I SAY —

SOME INK, PAPER, AND LIGHT! AND CONVEY WHAT I WILL SET DOWN TO MY LADY.

IT SHALL ADVANTAGE THEE MORE THAN EVER THE BEARING OF LETTER DID.

WHERE'S ANTONIO, THEN?

I COULD NOT FIND HIM AT THE ELEPHANT.

HIS COUNSEL NOW MIGHT DO ME GOLDEN SERVICE.

I AM READY TO DISTRUST MINE EYES AND WRANGLE WITH MY REASON THAT PERSUADES ME THAT I AM MAD...

OR ELSE THE LADY'S MAD!

NOW GO WITH ME AND THIS HOLY MAN.

PLIGHT ME THE FULL ASSURANCE OF YOUR FAITH,

THAT MY JEALOUS AND DOUBTFUL SOUL MAY LIVE AT PEACE.

WHAT DO YOU SAY?

I'LL GO WITH YOU...

AND, HAVING SWORN TRUTH, EVER WILL BE TRUE.

BELONG YOU TO THE LADY OLIVIA, FRIENDS?

AY, SIR, WE ARE SOME OF HER TRAPPINGS.

THERE'S GOLD. IF YOU WILL LET YOUR LADY KNOW I AM HERE TO SPEAK WITH HER...

AND BRING HER ALONG WITH YOU, IT MAY AWAKE MY BOUNTY FURTHER.

SIR, LULLABY YOUR BOUNTY TILL I COME AGAIN!

HERE COMES THE MAN THAT DID RESCUE ME.

THAT FACE I DO REMEMBER WELL...

YET WHEN I SAW IT LAST, IT WAS BESMEARED IN THE SMOKE OF WAR.

SHOVE

THIS IS ANTONIO THAT TOOK THE *PHOENIX* AND DID THE *TIGER* BOARD WHEN YOUR NEPHEW TITUS LOST HIS LEG.

HE DID ME KINDNESS, SIR... BUT PUT STRANGE SPEECH UPON ME.

KSH

FOR HIS SAKE DID I EXPOSE MYSELF TO THE DANGER OF THIS ADVERSE TOWN.

HIS FALSE CUNNING DENIED ME MINE OWN PURSE, WHICH I HAD RECOMMENDED TO HIS USE NOT HALF AN HOUR BEFORE.

HOW CAN THIS BE?

WHEN CAME HE TO THIS TOWN?

TODAY, MY LORD.

AND FOR THREE MONTHS BEFORE, BOTH DAY AND NIGHT DID WE KEEP COMPANY.

WHERE GOES CESARIO?

AFTER HIM I LOVE MORE THAN I LOVE MY LIFE...

MORE THAN EVER I SHALL LOVE WIFE.

AH ME, HOW AM I BEGUILED!

WHO DOES BEGUILE YOU?

HAST THOU FORGOT THYSELF?

IS IT SO LONG?

CALL FORTH THE HOLY FATHER!

FATHER, I CHARGE THEE TO UNFOLD WHAT HATH PASSED BETWEEN THIS YOUTH AND ME.

A CONTRACT OF ETERNAL BOND OF LOVE.

CONFIRMED SINCE BUT TWO HOURS.

O, THOU DISSEMBLING CUB!

FAREWELL, AND TAKE HER.

BUT DIRECT THY FEET WHERE THOU AND I HENCEFORTH MAY NEVER MEET.

MY LORD, I DO PROTEST —

LADY, YOU HAVE BEEN MISTOOK.

YOU ARE BETROTHED BOTH TO A MAID AND MAN.

IF THIS BE SO, I SHALL HAVE SHARE IN THIS MOST HAPPY WRECK.

BOY, THOU HAST SAID TO ME A THOUSAND TIMES, THOU NEVER SHOULD LOVE WOMAN LIKE TO ME.

AND ALL THOSE SAYINGS WILL I KEEP AS TRUE.

The twins Viola and Sebastian, all but identical in appearance, are shipwrecked on the shores of Illyria, each thinking the other dead. Thrown upon her own resources, Viola disguises herself as a boy (calling herself Cesario) and presents herself for service at the court of Duke Orsino – with whom she promptly falls in love. But Orsino is carrying a torch for his neighbour, the Countess Olivia, who is in mourning for her dead brother and uninterested in Orsino's tiresome attentions. Living under Olivia's roof are two people who cordially detest each other: her uncle, the feckless alcoholic Sir Toby Belch; and her butler, the puritanical Malvolio, who is himself hopelessly smitten with her. Impressed by the qualities of "Cesario" (i.e. the disguised Viola), Orsino sends him/her as a go-between to Olivia's household, but his plan misfires: Viola/Cesario's eloquent pleading on his behalf leads to Olivia falling in love, not with Orsino, but with Viola/Cesario herself.

Meanwhile, Sir Toby has been cynically cultivating the friendship of a rich aristocrat, the cowardly Sir Andrew Aguecheek, falsely promising *him* the hand-in-marriage of his niece. With the help of three of Olivia's servants – the feisty maid Maria, the resourceful Fabian, and Feste her household jester – a plot is successfully hatched to engineer the downfall of the hated Malvolio by forging a letter to him from Olivia, in which she apparently declares her love for him: when Malvolio acts on this letter, dressing in an incongruously flamboyant style and grinning at Olivia, he is declared mad.

This whirlwind of unrequited love is at last resolved by the appearance of Viola's "lost" twin, Sebastian, who, immediately falling in love with Olivia, prompts a series of misunderstandings and quarrels. Following the twins' joyful reunion, both Viola and Orsino, and Sebastian and Olivia, are free to declare their love – but others are left out in the cold. Sir Toby violently falls out with the cowardly Sir Andrew, who leaves for home after a farcical duel with Viola and a more violent offstage encounter with Sebastian; Antonio, the sea-captain who has adoringly steered Sebastian to this outcome, is now abandoned; Malvolio is released from his confinement, but vows revenge; and Feste the fool is left alone to sing the last of his sad songs.

A BRIEF LIFE OF WILLIAM SHAKESPEARE

Shakespeare's birthday is traditionally said to be the 23rd of April – St George's Day, patron saint of England. A good start for England's greatest writer. But that date and even his name are uncertain. He signed his own name in different ways. "Shakespeare" is now the accepted one out of dozens of different versions.

He was born at Stratford-upon-Avon in 1564, and baptized on 26th April. His mother, Mary Arden, was the daughter of a prosperous farmer. His father, John Shakespeare, a glove-maker, was a respected civic figure – and probably also a Catholic. In 1570, just as Will began school, his father was accused of illegal dealings. The family fell into debt and disrepute.

Will attended a local school for eight years. He did not go to university. The next ten years are a blank filled by suppositions. Was he briefly a Latin teacher, a soldier, a sea-faring explorer? Was he prosecuted and whipped for poaching deer?

We do know that in 1582 he married Anne Hathaway, eight years his senior, and three months pregnant. Two more children – twins – were born three years later but, by around 1590, Will had left Stratford to pursue a theatre career in London. Shakespeare's apprenticeship began as an actor and "pen for hire".

He learned his craft the hard way. He soon won fame as a playwright with often-staged popular hits.

He and his colleagues formed a stage company, the Lord Chamberlain's Men, which built the famous Globe Theatre. It opened in 1599 but was destroyed by fire in 1613 during a performance of *Henry VIII* which used gunpowder special effects. It was rebuilt in brick the following year.

Shakespeare was a financially successful writer who invested his money wisely in property. In 1597, he bought an enormous house in Stratford, and in 1608 became a shareholder in London's Blackfriars Theatre. He also redeemed the family's honour by acquiring a personal coat of arms.

Shakespeare wrote over 40 works, including poems, "lost" plays and collaborations, in a career spanning nearly 25 years. He retired to Stratford in 1613, where he died on 23rd April 1616, aged 52, apparently of a fever after a "merry meeting" of drinks with friends. Shakespeare did in fact die on St George's Day! He was buried "full 17 foot deep" in Holy Trinity Church, Stratford, and left an epitaph cursing anyone who dared disturb his bones.

There have been preposterous theories disputing Shakespeare's authorship. Some claim that Sir Francis Bacon (1561–1626), philosopher and Lord Chancellor, was the real author of Shakespeare's plays. Others propose Edward de Vere, Earl of Oxford (1550–1604), or, even more weirdly, Queen Elizabeth I. The implication is that the "real" Shakespeare had to be a university graduate or an aristocrat. Nothing less would do for the world's greatest writer.

Shakespeare is mysteriously hidden behind his work. His life will not tell us what inspired his genius.

EDITORIAL

Richard Appignanesi: Text Adaptor

Richard Appignanesi was a founder and co-director of the Writers & Readers Publishing Cooperative and Icon Books where he originated the internationally acclaimed *Introducing* series. His own best-selling titles in the series include *Freud*, *Postmodernism* and *Existentialism*. He is also the author of the fiction trilogy *Italia Perversa* and the novel *Yukio Mishima's Report to the Emperor*. Currently associate editor of the journal *Third Text* and reviews editor of the journal *Futures*, his latest book *What do Existentialists Believe?* was released in 2006.

Nick de Somogyi: Textual Consultant

Nick de Somogyi works as a freelance writer and researcher, as a genealogist at the College of Arms, and as a contributing editor to *New Theatre Quarterly*. He is the founding editor of the *Globe Quartos* series, and was the visiting curator at Shakespeare's Globe, 2003–6. His publications include *Shakespeare's Theatre of War* (1998), *Jokermen and Thieves: Bob Dylan and the Ballad Tradition* (1986), and (from 2001) the *Shakespeare Folios* series for Nick Hern Books. He has also contributed to the Open University (1995), Carlton Television (2000), and BBC Radio 3 and Radio 4.

ARTIST

Nana Li

Nana Li is a UK-based illustrator and comic artist, with a degree in engineering. Her prime source of inspiration has always been manga or manga-influenced art, although she also finds inspiration in games, movies, fashion, culture, concept and classical art. Nana runs workshops on manga and comic creation for libraries, schools and events in the UK. Nana's work has been published in the manga anthology *Mammoth's Book of Best New Manga 2* and was one of the winning entries in NEO Magazine 2007 competition. She is the grand prize winner of Tokyopop's Rising Stars of Manga UK & Ireland 3. Among some of her favourite comics are *Sanctuary*, *Naruto*, *Bleach* and *Rin!*.

PUBLISHER

SelfMadeHero is a UK-based manga and graphic novel imprint, reinventing some of the most important works of European and world literature. In 2008 SelfMadeHero was named **UK Young Publisher of the Year** at the prestigious British Book Industry Awards.

OTHER SELFMADEHERO TITLES:

EYE CLASSICS: *Nevermore*, *The Picture of Dorian Gray*, *The Trial*, *The Master and Margarita*, *Crime and Punishment*, *Dr. Jekyll and Mr. Hyde.*

SELF MADE HERO

www.selfmadehero.com